STANDING ON ONE LEG IS HARD

ERIKA McGANN
ILLUSTRATED BY CLIVE McFARLAND

THE O'BRIEN PRESS
DUBLIN

First published 2023 by The O'Brien Press Ltd,
12 Terenure Road East, Rathgar, Dublin 6, D06 HD27, Ireland
Tel: +353 1 4923333; Fax: +353 1 4922777
E-mail: books@obrien.ie
Website: obrien.ie
The O'Brien Press is a member of Publishing Ireland.
Copyright for text © Erika McGann
Copyright for illustrations © Clive McFarland
The moral rights of the author and illustrator have been asserted.
Design © The O'Brien Press 2023
Design and layout by Emma Byrne

ISBN: 978-1-78849-321-5

8 7 6 5 4 3 2 1
27 26 25 24 23

Printed and bound in Poland by Białostockie Zakłady Graficzne S.A.
The paper in this book is produced using pulp from managed forests.

Standing On One Leg is Hard receives financial assistance from The Art Council

ERIKA McGANN is the author of numerous children's
books, including the picture books *Where Are You Puffling?*
(illustrated by GERRY DALY) and *The Night-time Cat and the
Plump, Grey Mouse* (illustrated by LAUREN O'NEILL).

CLIVE MCFARLAND was raised in Omagh, County Tyrone
and graduated from Liverpool School of Art and Design.
He is an author and illustrator of picture books, including *A
Bed for Bear*, *Caterpillar Dreams* and *The Fox and the Wild*.
He lives in Northern Ireland.

Published in
DUBLIN
UNESCO
City of Literature

Growing up with
O'BRIEN
obrien.ie

Here is a heron,
tall and graceful,
standing on one leg.

Here is a heron chick,
short and fluffy.

SPLASH!

Standing on one leg is HARD.

What if she rests her foot on this rock?

SPLISH, SPLASH!

Nope.

A smaller chick might be useful.

SPLASH, SPLASH!

Nopedy-nope.

Sorry.

She could flap her wings to stay up.
That should work.

SPLASH!

Uh-uh.

What is the trick?

How do they do it?

It must be magic.

Is it best to stand on a stone?

All alone?

In the water?

On an otter?

Should she stick her beak in the air?

Or use a chair?

Ask a swan?

Put shoes on?

21

She could try them all at once.

It's no use.

She's tried and tried.

It's just too hard.

Unless ...

She thinks she knows.

She's pretty sure.

She's worked it out.

27

If YOU don't look,
she won't fall in.

So close your eyes.

She's got it now!

She's on one leg.

You didn't see?

Well, take a look ...